f1

This one is for Buster and Charlie.

The Quiet Pines Cemetery is just north of Hollywood, tucked away between two strip malls and a parking facility near Victory Boulevard. It's small and only the tiny crematorium in the back is still accepting business. It's got a Saltillo tile gate that's probably worth more than anything within the stone wall fencing, and there's talk of selling the land and moving the plots, but like much in Hollywood, nothing is happening in a hurry.

It's unofficially known as the Second Banana Cemetery, thanks to the many minor players and actors interred there. The major stars of the movies have always preferred Hollywood Forever, or Forest Lawn for their final resting spots, filling the favored gardens of repose and leaving precious little room there for the others who helped them in their rise to fame. For *those* folks— the straight men, the comic relief, the sidekicks and minor characters—they had Quiet Pines.

Wander these scraggly grounds and you'll find markers dating from the early Twenties all the way to the Eighties, with names that sound vaguely familiar. Some stones are crumbling and falling apart while others are metal plaques made to withstand the weather. Very, very few have flowers or visitors on a regular basis, and it shows. The only section that has any schedule of care is the one with the veterans; every second week in November and last week in May, those graves sport small American flags, provided and apathetically placed by the local boy scout troop for badge merit over patriotism.

--ooO0Ooo--

Los Angeles Times, June fifteenth, 1922

New Cemetery Opens

Quiet Pines, the new ten-acre cemetery built by the Novak Brothers will begin services today with the funeral and interment of actor Paul Seagan. Quiet Pines, which is located north of Santa Monica Blvd at Crescent Heights, has lovely lawns and a marble columbarium done in Greco-Roman style.

The Novaks hope to provide the community with a range of affordable and respectful burial services. For further information they ask you to contact them at 15699 Del Lirio Road, or Tel. HOL 8227.

1920s

Sheila Lawton

Born 1904—Died 1924

One out of a hundred, I knew the odds. Packed up my cardboard suitcase anyway and caught the early train out of a little nothing town on the outskirts of Cincinnati.

 I had the gams and the guts to make it in Hollywood, or so I thought. I was the lead in every play our school put on, and already knew how to deal with roving hands and sweet nothings. Girls learn early, and Mama didn't raise a pushover.

But a girl's gotta eat too, and sometimes that meant a distasteful compromise here and there. A kiss for a better line; a mauling for a walk-on. Sometimes the couch is the only seat at the table, you know?

And at some point, you realize it's the *only* seat you're being offered now.

I wonder if Reuben Meyer regrets the mess I left behind as much as I do.

I hope he does.

Edith Munro

"Our Lamb"

Born 1902—Died 1927

Pretty, but not pretty enough. The girl in the background of a dozen scenes, a hundred flickers. A guest here, another customer there . . . I stood or sat, laughed or watched . . . whatever Mr. Lee wanted.

And when all the other extras bitched about the gallons of cold water and lousy conditions on set, I gritted my teeth and made myself stay through every take of *The Perilous Sea*, knowing it was going to be a masterpiece.

I was right. Three Oscars, a full-page spread in all the papers.

The pneumonia took me in three days.

Macaulay Lee

"Director Extraordinaire"

Born 1884—died 1929

Art.

It's all I wanted to make, all my life. I spent years trying to draw to no avail, and music wasn't within me. But between a love of theater and a few connections there I found the perfect medium behind a 16-millimeter Bell and Howell camera.

Love stories. Chases. Dramatic revelations and relationships. Through the lens I composed for the public these two-reel tales touching on every emotion I could pull from my performers.

Love, hate, revenge, regret, betrayal, and confession. Folks said that a Macaulay Lee picture had it all and I gave it all, again and again. Each movie took a piece of me and by the time the studio agreed to let me do *The Citadel* I wasn't sure I could.

But the show must go on, and it did. Later, after the reviews were out it was easier to announce my retirement and settle into my Craftsman bungalow, drinking and waiting for the sting of humiliation to die.

I died first, though, drunkenly tumbling into my pool on a sunny California morning to be found floating later by my housekeeper, who cried before calling the tabloids and negotiating an exclusive.

Isaiah Henderson

Born 1886—Died 1925

I lost the coin toss, and Billy thought it was a damned hoot, but I figured I'd show him and all the rest of 'em how to take a fall with a horse and make it look good.

We had to put the mare down afterwards, though and I felt bad about that because she'd been a good one. When we loaded her remains into the truck, I got a little scraped up, but didn't think much of it. Who does? You spend months fallin' and fighting all to make a paycheck and for what? To have some damned doctor tell you it's tetanus. Terminal.

Goddamn it.

Reuben Meyer

"Rest in Peace"

Born 1866—Died 1929

I should have stayed in Newark. But ambition always got the better of me, so I came out to California late but full of ideas and plans to get ahead in the movie-making business. A side-step from theaters, but with more sunshine and young blondes.

Comedies and Westerns brought 'em in. My Sterling Studios cranked out pictures like goodies on a conveyor belt and the money rolled in. Then I bought theaters and sent flowers to certain reporters for good press and sent a few snoops around the other studios to take notes and dig dirt.

Hollywood's a small town. I knew about Buddy Howell's young busboy fixation, and Louis Atwill's chronic gambling, about how Gus Oakes over at Halcyon was chumming up to the local politicians in hopes of getting some slack on his union busting tactics. Good, useful information.

Just business, as the saying goes.

And then Sheila Lawton had to go and shoot herself in my bathroom, all because I wouldn't cast her in *Barbary Ladies*.

Finances, logistics, production schedules, supplies--all of those I understand as only the head of a studio can. But women? Who knows what goes through in their heads?

Besides bullets, that is.

I didn't last long after that scandal brought down Sterling Studios. One stroke led to another, and right before Black Friday, I bowed out.

Sidney March

Born 1886—died 1928

I was blessed with my mother's complexion and smile; gentle and warm. From my father I received broad shoulders and a certain stance that gave me enough presence to do well on the stages of Chicago.

Hollywood came calling and seduced, I moved west to star in bedroom dramas and historical fiction, playing the lead opposite the beauties of the day. The money was good, and in every interview, I made it a point to say I hadn't found the right woman yet.

Oh Lysander, I wish the world was kinder to us. At least you survived the crash. Think kindly of me once in a while, my love.

1930s

Phillip Harrison III

Born 1894--Died 1942

Born and bred on Albion's shores, I put my time in on the boards, as the rhyme goes. Everything from Shakespeare to Ibsen to Voltaire with the same attention to detail, the same love of theatre with only a small, ghastly intermission from '14 to '18 that still had me waking up once or twice a month, screaming.

But Alice wished for more, so we came to Hollywood, looking for work. They told her 'No thank you' but promptly put me in half a dozen films of dubious design. I was by turns a pirate, a general, a millionaire and a under it all, vastly amused. They paid for my accent by the vowel and while I soaked up the attention, Alice wanted to return to England.

I agreed to the divorce, both from her and my native soil, well aware of the small society of fellow ex-pats in Hollywood, and how we tolerated each other and our self-imposed exile. Cliques within cliques, circles and circles. Small, but a known quality.

There was more to it; there always is. I was in no hurry to be drafted to fight that rotten blighter in Germany, not after the first war. Ironically the studio sent me on a goodwill tour and our damned plane went straight into a snowy Nevada mountainside.

Jessie & Bessie Green

"Borne home on the wings of Angels"

Born 1904—died 1934

Born 1904—died 1948

We sang. Morning and night, at church, at school, at weddings. Most folks tossed coins when we did the old favorites, and when Ben played the fiddle, it added a real sweetness to anything we sang.

Halcyon Studios hired us to do songs for one of their pictures and so we did, singing up a storm for *Sally's Shiloh Days* and *Sacramento Trail.* We didn't know how to read music, but if we heard a tune a few times, we could sing it, harmonize to it and generally make it ours. Had a good time until the studio told us we couldn't sing anywhere but with them.

Well, that didn't sit right. God gave us the pipes to make music, and we were gonna do it no matter what Mr. Wright or anybody said. We got talked to, and warned and finally they cut our contract, saying we were 'unable to take direction.'

We took our money and went home to Victorville. Jessie passed into the everlovin' arms of the Lord when she got diphtheria, and Bessie followed of a heart attack years later. Since the plots were paid for, we ended up here.

Neither of us regrets a thing.

--ooOOoo--

Los Angeles Times July 10th, 1937

FIRE THREATENS HOMES, CEMETERY

Hollywood Ca—

A fast-moving brush fire has left devastation across fifty acres in its wake so far as it raced through the hills and heights of Hollywood. Fire crews have been working overnight to keep the flames from reaching the bottom of Laurel Canyon. Fire Chief Royal Hastings urges the public to stay alert and be ready to vacate if the notorious Santa Ana winds continue through the evening.

Currently the fire line is just north of the Quiet Pines Cemetery, having burned through Spaulding Square and parts of the canyons therein.

--ooOOoo--

Noble Dumont

Born 1861—died 1937

At the start I did it all—needed someone to take a pratfall? Me. Someone needed to haul the camera from one place to another?

Me. Building sets, driving actors, running errands, most of us just pitched in to get it done. When I got promoted in '26 to cameraman, I was pleased as punch. Worked with some of the best, both in front and behind the lens.

I musta filmed over a hundred and forty pictures, cranking them out from the two-reeler chases all the way to screwballs and I learned early on that you can't make a good picture from a bad script. When I told Aaron Wright that his story for *Sailor's Luck* sucked donkey balls, he fired me off the picture that afternoon. What the fuck did *I* know about good writing, he wanted to know. I was just a damned Okie cameraman who'd never been to college.

But the box office returns proved me right, though. Wright had to eat a lot of crow over that. Of course, I was stupid and shot my mouth off, so when he showed up at the Sudsy Barrel with two fists and murder in his eyes, we got into it. By the time the cops drove up, I was beating Aaron over the head with a broken barstool while the photographers and reporters were taking bets.

Might not have been to college, but I could always hold my own in any bar fight.

Sentenced to ten years for aggravated assault even though the fucker jumped ME. Got out of Folsom after six years, but by then my TB had flared up bad and my days were numbered. Bought myself a space here when the place was first being built.

That's all I got to say about that.

Margaret "Margie" Thayer

Born 1887—Died 1939

When you go to the movies, you want to see lives that are prettier than your own. You want to see palaces and princesses instead of the real world—that's the magic. My part in making that began with needle and thread.

I started under Madame Clarine, sewing coats for extras. When she found out I could handle a machine I got moved to the primary casts which meant measurements and fittings and shopping for fabrics and deadlines and re-fittings and fussing, fighting, and fury, not necessarily in that order. Some stars will not accept that they've gained weight. Some stars will not accept that red isn't their color, or velvet doesn't photograph well.

The truth is that some stars are idiots.

I digress. For every hothouse flower there IS a gracious soul who takes direction and actually cares about what they wear both in front of and away from the camera. Like that lovely Mr. March. Or Miss Del Marr, who looked divine in nearly everything.

Of course, I also knew exactly why some stars needed a few extra inches and sometimes, in a quiet desperate moment, they would ask if I knew anybody. Anybody who could help them . . . lose a little around the middle. Sometimes the star breaks down or looks so sad or scared that you can't imagine they're the same one in front of the camera, smiling radiantly in some picture.

I would slip them a card for Doctor Holloway and say something about how he's the soul of discretion, and conveniently close to the studios . . . poor girls.

Your money or your life . . . seems like the studio always wanted both.

Aaron Wright

"Writer and Friend to All"

Born 1870—died 1938

A degree from Yale, a distinguished stint at Vanity Fair and for what? Long days trying to sort literary wheat from chaff while dealing with the idiots within the studio. Nobody ever appreciated the amount of bovine excrement I had to wade through to get a decent picture made.

Oh, we had good source material at times, and a few crackerjack writers but the grind of churning out the scripts was brutal. I think in all of '32, I might have been home maybe six times in all? Hard to remember; the years blur even as you recollect the ache in your shoulders and the bone weariness at the end of the day, curling up on the office sofa because you're too drunk or too tired to make it home.

So, when that stupid hick camera ape starts shooting off his mouth, I blow. Never mind that he's got a point—*Sailor's Luck* was no Pulitzer Prize winner, yeah, yeah—it's the principle of the thing. That, and a need to thump somebody once in a while because around here, tempers flare hard and hot, buddy.

I ended up losing an eye, a couple of molars and my job. Slunk my way back East to drink away my pains while avoiding all calls. Within a few years my whole world centered on those bottles of sweet brown relief as my liver slowly calcified and my brain softened like gum on a summer sidewalk.

40s

Augustus "Gus" Oaks

Born 1875—Died 1944

My father was a theater manager, my mother a star. I knew firsthand what a scam 'entertainment' was and kept that to myself even as I built Halcyon Studios in 1919 from the ground up. Nobody poured more into it than I did, from hiring the best to keeping them in line, my gut dissolving itself in ulcers even as we made a profit.

Scandals, hits, box office poison, rumors, outrage, packed houses—these were the way of it and I took them all on, keeping the name of Halcyon high and bright. We had the prettiest starlets, the wittiest pictures, the glamor America needed, damn it! I wasn't going to be second-best to anyone, let alone that bastard Meyer over at Sterling, let me tell you.

When the pressure got too much, I'd drive over to a certain mansion in Holmby Hills and spend some time with a few 'friends' just relaxing. Nothing illegal about a little face powder and some heels to feel better.

Got us through the Crash and cranked up the comedies to help people forget their troubles even as the Hays Office started snipping about how long kisses could be, and not showing bedrooms in pictures. Sanctimonious pricks, all of them, with no idea how *much* Mr. and Mrs. America wanted to see all the details.

Then the war started, and the government wanted patriotic movies, all the better to keep people buying bonds, and cutting into our profits. Between trying to keep my producers and investors happy, I lost hair, weight, and patience. My top Limey star died in a plane crash, I tried to squash rumors about MDM running around with some unsavory characters and to top it all, the last party at the house in Holmby Hills got raided by the Vice Squad.

I paid to keep my name out of the papers, but they kept demanding more, and good as Halcyon was doing, there was a bottom to the piggy bank. When nobody else in town would take my calls, that prick Neil Henninger from Atlantis Pictures sailed in with a last-minute offer we both knew was as insulting as it was unavoidable.

The publicity department announced I was 'overworked' and 'heading out of town for a much-needed rest' but that got dropped a few weeks after they found what was left of me washing up on Pismo Beach.

--oo0Ooo--

Los Angeles Times, November 29th, 1944

INCIDENT AT QUIET PINES

Los Angeles, Ca—

A minor incident yesterday marred the interment of Augustus 'Gus' Oaks, the former head of Halcyon Studios. According to witnesses at the graveside service, a veiled woman in attendance began shouting accusations at Neil Henninger, head of Atlantis Studios before assaulting him with her handbag.

Mr. Henninger attempted to defend himself and fell into the grave, sustaining minor injuries after landing on the coffin and upsetting several floral tributes in the process. The unknown woman left the scene before the police arrived, and Mr. Henninger was taken to St. Vincent Hospital for treatment and released. He has refused to press charges.

--oo0Ooo--

Lysander Vincent

"Ever Faithful unto Death"

Born 1887-Died 1947

My work was the only thing that kept me going after dear Sidney passed away. Every day I'd come in and select pieces or help create pieces for whatever the studio needed. Short interludes? Musical cues for a shift of pace? A theme to associate with the heroine? My forte.

Back when the pictures were silent, I helped compile the reams of sheet music that accompanied the reels on their way to the theaters, knowing that some small-town pianist or organist would be following along with the images above them. I tried to make it easy.

Later, when sound was here to stay, I worked with the in-house musicians almost exclusively, building a library of pieces. Ever since the accident I walked with a cane, but the offices were all on the first floor, so I was spared the indignity of pulling myself up and down the stairs under those pitying gazes . . . at least before the big renovations. Then the Music department got sent out to Glendora—Glendora! And I found myself forced to commute for the first time in my life.

The pains got worse as the years rolled by, and I came to rely more and more on the sweet morphine to get through the days. Finally, when I realized I had neither my darling Sidney nor a life worth anything, I laid myself to rest with a triple dose. The papers were discreet, calling it 'accidental' but a few of you know the truth.

Be kind, my friends; it's all we have in this life.

Mary Del Marr

Born 1904—Died 1948

A little taller, a little thinner, a little blonder, a little quieter— nothing ever made them happy. Not the thousands of dollars my pictures made, not the thousands of fan letters and clubs across the country. I let them put me in heels, watch my calories, bleach my hair and coach my speech, all to transform from meek, mousy Mable Dykowski into marvelous, magnificent Mary Del Marr.

What a load of crap.

But I had people counting on me: Ma and Sally mostly, with money going out to my Uncle Jack and the cousins in Indiana as well. I could make more in a week than all six of them combined, and family's family when you're a Dykowski.

Even the biggest cash cow can be bled to death by enough parasites, though. Everyone taking their little piece, reassuring me it wasn't much, I could spare it, right? I tried not to begrudge them, but it was clear to me they were never going to stop the grift. Not even Ma, who loved me even as she cashed my paychecks right out of my pocketbook.

So, after a decade of hard work with barely any savings to show for it, I balked. I deliberately set Artie Van Cliff and Ricardo Ibarra at each other's throats over Cathy; drank like a sailor in all the best nightclubs; got thrown out of a lot of the worst ones. I showed up late, let myself get arrested a few times, and when Gus Oakes had enough, he fired me.

I went looking for a place to end it all, so I drove up to La Habra around some of the quiet acres up there. God it was gorgeous, and I sort of took my time along those meandering roads. Then I spotted a 'For Sale' sign and that afternoon, I bought an avocado farm under my real name. Ma was pissed and took Sally home to Indiana, calling me an ungrateful bitch but I didn't care. I got a few dogs and sold crop after crop to the produce buyers for all those LA restaurants. That last fancy salad of yours probably had one of my big, glorious Hass in it.

Those years in La Habra were the best years of my life, and I don't regret making that change, not even when I gently dropped dead of a heart attack between two trees in the orchard one October morning.

Lian "Lenny" Chen

Born 1877—Died 1939

My grandfather came from the homeland to work on the railroads. He and my father went on to build houses, farms, and stores all around Los Angeles. I worked with them until the day some white men came to film part of a movie nearby. I went to watch. The poorly constructed storefront kept wobbling, so I took it upon myself to stabilize it with loose wood.

One of the men saw me do it, and I was worried I would be beaten, but instead, he asked me if I understood English, and if I could do the same to the other side of the storefront. I could and I did, so that was the start of working for Atlantis Studios.

It was hard and long, but I enjoyed seeing my work on the screen—first outdoor sets, like cabins and bridges, but later, I was promoted and helped to build more elaborate sets of castles, palaces, grand staircases and elegant interiors. I learned about lighting and décor and different time periods with their details. So much going on all the time!

The studio would not pay me as much as the white workers and tried to tell me it was the law. I lied to them that two of the other studios wanted me to go work for them, and much as I loved

Atlantis, I had a growing family to feed. They fretted about it for a few days, and I finally received almost 5 dollars a day more, with a warning that it would not happen again. I agreed, for I had seen other men fired, beaten, or worse, just for asking.

Still, I fared compared to many others around me. I always had work, and I enjoyed creating sets. My wife and I saved to put both our sons through college, and I lived long enough to see my first granddaughter born. When the time came, I asked for a place here, among the others who worked at bringing a little joy into the world.

I rest well.

Wilbur Zythros

Born 1887—Died 1937

I never meant to kill her. God as my witness, I didn't. Things got out of hand, and between the booze and the pills, none of us were innocent. *The Wild Seas* had been a hard shoot, what with the studio breathing down my neck, and the accounting office wanting receipts for every damned thing. A director gets it from both barrels with the front office and the studio. When it was time to wrap, I wanted the best scotch in unlimited amounts and got it, too.

We laughed it up at Guido's and at closing, I suggested taking the good times back to my place, they agreed, climbing into my

Packard and whooping it up. I thought everybody was in and started to back up, only to mow down Sadie right there in the parking lot, crushing her against the bricks of the restaurant.

Jesus, her scream!

The law called it 'accidental manslaughter' and I got three years for it. I did my time because I deserved it, but I never slept a full night afterwards, and no studio would hire me, not while the papers were calling me a murderer. Best I could do were some documentary shorts under another name, for chicken scratch.

One mistake. That's all it takes to be thrown out with the garbage in this town. One stupid misjudgment on my part and it's all anyone will remember me for. Forget all those years of good pictures—I'll always be 'that director who ran over the actress.'

50s

Neil Henninger

"Devoted Father and Husband"

Born 1901—Died 1957

The best way to make it to the top at a studio is to marry into it. I was a junior leading man who married Reuben Meyer's ugly daughter just in time to take the attention off his scandal with the dead starlet in his bathroom. Stepping over bodies is a way of life in Hollywood, believe me, and I have long legs.

Rachel understood the deal, and after I got her pregnant, we settled into an understanding, the way so many upwardly mobile couples do. I'd run the studio, and she was free to ignore the reports of my infidelity while raising our daughter and doing all that country club shit that's so popular with the wives of important men.

I scooped up Halcyon in '44, expanding Atlantis by almost a third, and when some of my development men started talking about television, I was listening. Not ready to throw any money at it, but it never hurt to lend a few stars out and see what the public thought. Then the war was over and suddenly nobody wanted patriotic pictures, now it was all about bugs and monsters.

Giant ants, giant spiders, giant this and that. The public wanted to be scared and we accommodated them, making them bigger and louder than anybody else's out there. I hired writers nobody else wanted and squeezed them for all I could get, which was mostly Science Fiction. A couple of them turned in some dramas too, for the older folks not into bugs.

Yes, I had affairs, but they meant nothing—at least to me. But I guess after all the years they got to Rachel. She set me up with a gut full of whiskey and grease on the top three stairs, watching me fall and crack my skull on the marble floor of our foyer. I lost consciousness while she scrubbed the steps clean, talking to me about how she was going out for the evening to establish an alibi.

As I died, I considered who they'd cast when they made the movie of it all.

Cathy Arco

"Our Laughing Sweetheart"

1920-1953

It wasn't 'exhaustion.'

That's what they say when they need something to tell the papers. 'Exhaustion' is one. 'Flu' is another, and sometimes it's 'stomach issues,' but they're all euphemisms for the stuff the studios don't want to admit. For a lot of the fellahs it's drugs or booze. This town runs at a pace that will eat you alive, and to keep up you sometimes need a boost. Or two. Or more.

Gals have the added problems of Aunt Flo and her unpredictable schedule, natch. Isn't an actress out there who hasn't felt that dreaded trickle. Or even worse, *hasn't* felt it in a few months. The public loves us, but we're not allowed to be mothers, unless we do a big show of adopting, like Crawford did. Turn motherhood into a publicity stunt, rah, rah.

The problem is that real life doesn't work that way. Fun as Ricardo was, I wasn't about to marry him, and certainly I wasn't looking to have his kid. Unfortunately, my only option was to head to Tijuana and visit a certain house there for the afternoon.

My only memories are of the ceiling, and the pain.

Later, when I got back to LA, I thought I was going to be fine— that's what my friends told me. They'd been through worse, I was a trooper, all that song and dance but words didn't change the fact that I was a goner. No amount of last-minute penicillin could save me from the fatal infection eating me up from the inside out.

Botched. The survivors usually end up sterile. The unlucky ones-- like me--got buried.

Arthur VanCliff

"Pride of Saginaw"

1902-1958

I didn't start out planning to be an actor. Originally was going to be an accountant because I'd always had a head for numbers. In fact, I was doing taxes for most of the studio personnel when one morning I delivered something in person. I was grabbed, told to stand in the background for a scene and that was it— hooked. I had the height and a pretty good speaking voice, so

Atlantis put me in the stable. I did westerns and dramas and a comedy or two in the time I was with them.

Mostly they put me in pictures with Mary Del Marr, and she was a swell kid. Not my type, but fun to pal around with. Early on she figured out my deal but kept it quiet, so I owed her one for that. We got along fine until she started gossiping with Ricardo, one of the other box office draws from the other side of the studio. I'm not sure what she said to him about me, exactly, but it was enough to make Ricardo come storming over to the set of The Hour of Sunrise and start swinging at me.

It was a shit show, with the tabloids and columnists trying to get their digs in as well. Ricardo was already in their sights just for being Puerto Rican and dating white girls while I was getting slammed for three crappy pictures and a couple of speeding tickets. <u>Confidential</u> was getting close to the real mark though, and I knew if they published it, I was through. After all, look what they'd done to Rory and others with their exposés.

But it hit the newsstands within a week, and the studio dropped me, citing the bad publicity. Thank God I'd used my skill with numbers to make some smart investments, so money wasn't a problem. I settled in to let things blow over and within a few months Henninger's death took the attention off my disgrace long enough for me to start up my investment firm.

I missed the cameras and the glamor of course, but I had a house in on Roxbury Drive and a rolodex full of high-paying clients so I can't complain. Hell, I even helped Mary buy a farm in La

Habra, so no hard feelings there. No, if I had any regrets, it was probably not kicking the damned cigarettes. I ended up dying slowly from lung cancer as Sputnik raced overhead and the world panicked about it.

Ricardo Ibarra

"Reposar en Paz"

1904-1959

I was *muy* talented if I do say so myself. I could sing—in two languages! I could dance, I could act, and I wasn't hard to look at, judging by the box office returns. Sure, my skin was brown, and sure they wanted to change my name to Richard Barris but I said no, I'm not ashamed of my family.

They weren't too happy about that, and even less when I stole every picture I was in. I mean who could resist me? I put the snap in the snappy lines and the moves into every dance so I could win every heart out there, including Cathy Arco's. Ohhh that woman! She was everything I wanted: blonde, beautiful, and dynamite. I kept begging the studio to put us in a picture together, telling them we'd be a box office hit!

They never did. Something about a Latin man with a white woman put them off, even though I escorted half their stable to the clubs and bars most nights. I pushed harder, but it didn't happen, but after she and I got paired up to present at the Oscars. I made sure to play it up and it worked—she fell for me.

Or so I thought. After a few fun weeks, though, she wouldn't return my calls. Her secretary said that 'Miss Arco enjoyed your company but feels it's best to part as friends.' When I got in the woman's face, she added that it had been Mr. VanCliff's advice.

Sonofabitch! Bad enough that fruit was pals with Mary, but the idea that he'd gotten into my business with Cathy was too damned much. I lost my temper and let him have it but good.

Of course, the studio slammed us both, ordering me to lay low and cutting him loose right before the tabloids exposed Van Cliff for what he was. Bastard landed on his feet though, proving it's all about who you know in this town.

I did a few more pictures, mostly in supporting roles, and then the studio cut me loose. I went to television, picking up parts here and there, mostly second banana work not worthy of my talent. Started drinking, and after a while that was my full-time job. I ended up being shot during a liquor store robbery at Hollywood and Wilcox while picking up my weekly bottles of Muscatel.

When they told the punk gunman who I was, he'd never heard of me.

--ooo0ooo—

Los Angeles Times, July22nd, 1952

EARTHQUAKE IN KERN COUNTY

Los Angeles, Ca—

A strong earthquake rumbled through Kern County at four twenty-seven PM yesterday killing at least ten people and causing major damage to the towns of Tehachapi and Bakersfield. The mayor of Tehachapi, Gus Koutroulis, estimated the destruction repairs would ultimately top over a million dollars.

In Bakersfield, the earthquake disrupted pipelines and damaged several buildings. Fires flared up through the night, but crews were unable to pump water to douse the flames. The quake was felt as far north as Reno, and as far south as Tijuana Mexico. Here in Los Angeles, the damages are minor apart from the iconic Saltillo tile gate at Quiet Pines Cemetery in West Hollywood, which according to the Novak Brothers will have to be replaced.

Blossom Holly

1906-1960

I've always had a matronly look, even as a girl, and while Hollywood loves stars, they also need the supporting players to make those stars look good. I was the aunt, the older sister, the wisecracking secretary, the housekeeper, the best damned supporting player out there. I got to be the shoulder to cry on, the best friend who hears the confessions, and the mother who sends her boy off to war. I got to represent real people on the screen and that was just fine by me.

The nice part was that I grew into the roles, and because I was reliable, a lot of directors had me on their preferred hire lists. I was also good about keeping my mouth shut—not that any reporter ever wanted to interview ME—so if there was gossip about who was a Commie, or who did reefer, or who had something on the side, I didn't spill it. We all have our vices and lord knows this business is hard enough with seventeen-hour days and all.

It was a complete surprise when Magnus Isaacson fell for me.

This wasn't supposed to happen! He was ten years younger than I was and had all the makings of a leading man with that blonde hair and those big blue eyes. I thought for sure he'd be squiring our starlets but no, he spent more and more time with me during rehearsals. When I told him that he could do better than a middle-aged supporting player he just laughed.

"I don't think so. You're something the rest of them aren't, Blossom. You're *good*. You're good at what you do, but mostly you're a good person and in this town that is damned rare. That's why I adore you."

What girl could resist that? After dating a while, we eloped in Ensenada and spent fifteen glorious years together. Magnus got into directing and when he got the Oscar for his work on <u>The Trail of the Mohawks,</u> I clapped harder than anyone else in the theater.

We never did have children, but our friends did, and we spoiled them as much as we did our many, many pets. Magnus passed away of stomach cancer a few years before me and I mourned hard, aware of how lucky I had been to love and have been loved so well.

Sometimes dreams in Hollywood DO come true.

60s

Peachie Sandoval

1911-1967

I made *Rancho Solano* into a hit. Me, working like a dog from six in the morning until after ten each night. I worked and reworked scripts until the stories gleamed. Every character had their motivation, ever scene had its beat, its moment. I built the world and the families and the circus of emotions that made that show a hit. *Rancho Solano* was my baby.

Oh what's that? Where was I in the credits? Ahhh, funny thing that. Atlantis Productions was proud of what we'd done with their television division, but not quite ready to list a woman as head writer for a western, so I was listed as 'P. Sandoval' in the credits. All the other writers, directors and production staff got their full names, including the ladies in charge of wardrobe and make-up, but not me. Leonard Pellman, the executive in charge told me to my face that they couldn't list me because a name like Peachie would 'cast aspersions' on the 'rugged theme' of 'our beloved show.'

I shouldn't have cared. I was still getting paid—not as much as the men of course-- and I could still list *Rancho Solano* on my resume, but it pissed me off that I had to hide in plain sight that way, so I gave it a year, biding my time and writing specs and project outlines I figured I could pitch to Dulux, or if not them, then radio for sure.

When the fifth season of *Rancho Solano* ended, I had dinner with Pellman and laid it out for him: either I got credit by my full name and a bonus, or I would walk. Pellman laughed at first, and then got annoyed and angry when I wouldn't change my mind. He hemmed and hawed, said he'd have to discuss it with management. I told him to go ahead and do it. I refused to lose my temper and that just kept pissing him off.

"It's because you're a dyke, isn't it?" he kept jeering at me. "Hell of a thing with a name like Peachie. Should be Bitch."

"It's because I do damned good work and you know it, Len. Doesn't matter if I have tits or balls, I write a good show and I deserve more for it."

He fired me. Best thing that could have happened, because two weeks later I was sitting in the writer's room at Dulux, pitching my new series, *Sail to the Stars*.

Two Emmys, a Peabody award, and a lock on the Thursday night line-up for *seven years*, baby. When Dulux suggested spin-offs I was ready, and got to see three new shows spring from the original even as I got the test results from my doctor.

Pancreatic cancer.

So, I wrote faster, and longer, leaving a filing cabinet of scripts for the other writers, and even filming a goodbye for them and the cast, who had been the best damned family anyone could ask for.

In the end it was quick, but I did what I wanted to do, and that lets me rest easy. Stick to your guns, people—the satisfaction is worth the trouble.

Sandra Pitch

"Beloved daughter and star"

1932-1966

Mother was the one who wanted to be a star, not me. Growing up I heard all about her singing and dancing lessons, about her auditions and bit roles on Broadway. She kept reminding me I came from a talented family, and that performing was in the blood.

Maybe in her blood, but not mine. I'd shrink with embarrassment when she'd bully directors and the studio 'on my behalf' for better dressing rooms and larger parts. Maybe that's why people either loved me or hated me—it depended on whether they saw me as separate from her or not.

As I got older, I started putting my foot down, and that led to a few fights I can tell you. Mother insisted on treating me like a child even when I was wearing bras and towering over her. She'd scream if I suggested cutting my hair or driving myself somewhere without an escort. It got to the point where I was going nuts.

The voices kept telling me I didn't need her, and that she was the entire reason I was stuck playing walk-ons and secondaries. They urged me to get free, going from murmurs to full-on shouting in my head, giving me migraines and bloodshot eyes. I had trouble sleeping, and when I asked to see a doctor, Mother told me he'd only call me 'high-strung' and send me home again.

When I was fired from the set of *Spring in Seattle* for being tardy, Mother laid into me, berating me in front of the entire cast before smacking me in the face and hustling me out to the car.

Well, the voices were right, and later that night after I finished washing off the cleaver, I called the police and waited for them to come get me.

I liked Camarillo. They let me garden and read as long as I wanted. And the voices kept me company even when I caught pneumonia and drifted away one quiet night in November.

LT. Roger Chernov

US ARMY

1946-1976

It was just my luck to be drafted right when I was on the verge of a breakthrough. I'd done in time on commercials and auditions, and when Dulux was putting together a comedy that needed a wisecracking older son, I was in the right place but not at the right time.

My agent told me to go do my stint; he'd be waiting when I got back from Vietnam. He assured me that Elvis had survived a tour in the army, and I would too. "You'll be a hero to both the girls AND their parents!" he told me, which sounded good.

So, I reported to 4727 Wilshire Blvd along with hundreds of other guys to get processed and assigned. I was hoping for something in my line—maybe the Entertainment unit or USO liaison. Fat chance—they put me in Ordinance.

Two years later, I left my innocence behind in Vietnam, along with my right leg and bits of my skull. The VA did what they could, which helped, but nobody wanted to put a cripple on TV, and my agent wouldn't take my calls. Bastard.

I got mad. I could have let myself get maudlin and drink my sorrows away, but that wasn't the kind of guy I was. Instead, I started working with a local theater to put on productions using only handicapped actors. We didn't make a lot of money, but the audiences were supportive, and as more and more folks found us, we got big enough to get noticed by the studios.

DBNO theater, we called ourselves. Down But Not Out players. We visited schools and hospitals and churches. We got so big that my old agent called, and I won't lie—hanging up on HIM felt damned good. I sank my savings into a trust fund for the troupe and got us a terrific manager who had us doing all sorts of events to show that we were still great actors, even with disabilities.

I didn't expect the stroke, but between the cigarettes, the skull injury and the hypertension there you have it. I went quickly at least, and they left my chair on the side of the stage in memoriam on opening night of their new production.

Ed LaSalle

"Devoted husband and 'Papi"

1908-1969

I ran an RCA TK-40/41. That's a television camera and it's one big bastard, let me tell you. About three hundred pounds, and even now, it's not an easy thing to work with, nope. I was blessed with a longshoreman's build though, so I was able to wrangle it without too much trouble most of the time. Those of us on crew for Dulux Studios were expected not only to run our cameras, but also to do any quick repairs on them as needed because filming only stops for the major disasters, not the small ones.

I started under Butch Howland over at Opus Studios back when I was in high school in '26. I'd hustle over after classes and work as his assistant until after eight most nights, doing my homework between takes and breaks. Butch knew a hell of a lot about setting up, framing, and nailing the good shots. He would talk to each actress about what she wanted and worked with the director to reach some compromise. He gave me a letter of introduction so I could stop in at other studios and get a feel for their cameras. Eastman Kodak was the big name and I made it a point to learn them all as best I could.

Spent nearly thirty-five years filming from the day I was hired, and I've done them all. Love stories, westerns, dramas, comedies, mysteries. Directors counted on me, and I did my best to deliver. When the salesman from RCA came to town, I asked what sort of training they offered, and the answer floored me:

none. They only sold cameras, he told me. Studios already had trained cameramen.

I told my wife that seemed stupid, and that if the studio really wanted top-notch cameramen, they should set up a few courses, or have some sort of mentor program. I mean I'd lucked out in having Butch, but I was no spring chicken, and the cameras were getting fancier all the time, especially the ones for color film.

Charlie Quint over in the technical office thought it was a good idea and took it to the top, where they collaborated with the nearest college and within a year, they had a course and internships set up. In the first group though, there was a girl and I wasn't sure about that. How was a sweet little thing like Carla Petrosi gonna handle it? I told her I had my doubts about her handling cameras and what does she do?

A dolly. She gets a group of the guys to load the RCA TK-40/41 onto a rig dolly and it works. I'm watching her move the camera around like a *pro* and right then I know the program is bringing in the right people because even though Carla is only about five feet, she has the kind of confidence I would have killed for at the same age.

I invite her home to dinner.

Over the next few years, the wife and I watched her pick up the Oscar for Best Cinematography three times: for *The Fusion of Time,* for *Two Freeways to Chicago* and *Heart's Map.* Carla kept them at our house and came to dinner every Thursday for years until the wife and I moved into the MPTF old folks' home.

Sure, I'm proud of my work. But I'm *so* much prouder of Carla's by a long shot.

"Captain" Joe Hardwicke

1907-1970

Location scout. That's an official job now, but back when I started, it was just an added chore in a workday that started at dawn. I got into making movies waaay back then, and because I liked getting out and around, I knew the lay of the land pretty well. Grew up just south of Westmont myself and got to see a lot of changes.

There's a place up by the Hollywood sign for example, just to the north, before the Wonder View trail where Macaulay Lee filmed *Peaceful Days* with Carlotta Jones back in '26. Haven't been there in decades but I remember it well. Another spot is over by the Griffith Park Merry-go-Round's Fire Road, about fifty yards in, between a few Eucalyptus trees. It's pretty overgrown at times, and sometimes I worry about fire crews getting in there, especially during droughts, but so far it's fine.

Directors would tell me what they wanted: a lake for the background; a meadow; maybe some private beach—and I would find a spot for 'em. They trusted me to contact whoever owned the place and work out a deal with them. I was a smooth talker if I do say so myself, so there usually wasn't any trouble. And afterwards, when we'd hauled away the sets and taken down the fixtures, it would be empty . . . for a while.

I'd take dates to places where we'd filmed. I'd show them photos of the sets and get them to pose for me before . . . well, before the date ended. Those pictures were nice souvenirs and I kept them, so I'd remember. The only one I didn't keep was from that empty lot in Leimert Park, but it was okay because the newspapers and tabloids printed a few of her.

It's easy to get a date. Just tell girls you work for a studio and bam! just like that, even if you're as ugly as I am. Oh I know they were only using me just the way I was using them, but everyone plays the same game in the end, and most people lose, down the line. Me, I lost a few places, but that's because this town is getting bigger with developers and construction moving in.

The last one, though, was damned close. Down in Benedict Canyon, in August, as I recall. We'd shot a promo from one of the hillsides and it was a nice, secluded spot, so I kept it in mind.

I was cleaning things up when I heard a commotion from one of the houses down below. I didn't want trouble, so I went back to my truck and waited. Someone screamed but I kept still until I heard a car start up and leave. Later I read in the papers about what happened, and it hit me how close it had been, and how I could have gotten swept up with those hippies if I hadn't been smart.

The police checked on the studio. We told them we'd filmed here a few weeks before, so we all got dismissed as suspects and I didn't hear anything more. Went back after a few weeks to check on my last date and she was still there, safe and sound.

Then of all damned things, I choked to death on a veal cutlet over at Fannie's Famous Diner over on La Mirada, falling to the floor before any of the waitresses could call an ambulance. My favorite, Carole, stayed with me as I died right there on the linoleum, telling me to hold on even as I felt myself fade out and into blackness.

Los Angeles Times, September 12th, 1974

QUIET PINES TO DECLARE BANKRUPTCY

Quiet Pines, the ten-acre cemetery at Crescent Heights and Santa Monica has been struggling financially for the past decade due to a combination of poor management and questionable practices, according to Milton Hargreeves, the current director and caretaker.

"Unfortunately, the Novaks never set up any sort of perpetual care fund, and pocketed most of the income from the cemetery," Hargreeves said. "As a result, we've had a difficult time just running a day-to-day operation. That, along with the fact that we're just about full up is truth of it."

Quiet Pines, which opened in 1922, is one of the oldest cemeteries in Los Angeles and is set to close after New Years. Hargreeves is currently contacting families to make arrangements for relocating their loved ones.

www.ingramcontent.com/pod-product-compliance
Lightning Source LLC
Chambersburg PA
CBHW061645130726
47996CB00003B/1459